MW00908915

A Dinosaur Lives in Red Rock Canyon

By Marvin (Nick) Saines
Interpretive Naturalist - Geologist
Las Vegas, Nevada
greatunc@aol.com

Illustrated by Jonathan A. Kaplan
Kaplan Design Labs
Las Vegas, Nevada
jonakap1@gmail.com

TURTLEHEAD BOOKS

A Dinosaur Lives in Red Rock Canyon
Copyright © 2015 by Marvin (Nick) Saines
The author retains sole copyright.

ALL RIGHTS RESERVED

No part of this book may be reproduced or transmitted in any form, or by any electronic, mechanical, or other means, including photocopying, recording, or by information storage or retrieval systems, which includes unauthorized posting on the world wide web or internet in any form, without permission in writing from the publisher, except for brief quotations and selected artwork, embodied in literary articles or reviews.

First Turtlehead Books Edition 2015
10 9 8 7 6 5 4 3
Library of Congress Control Number: 2014922132

ISBN: 978-0-692-34912-0

Also by the author: *Geological Treasures of Red Rock Canyon*
(Available in 2018)

Turtlehead Books
1587 Figueroa Drive
Las Vegas, Nevada 89123 USA
702-896-4049
Greatunc@aol.com

Dedicated to future dinosaur hunters:

Sophie Rebecca Saines

Ryan Zachary Saines

and

James Vansen Saines

It hardly ever rains in the Mojave Desert. In fact, the Mojave is the driest desert in the country. But in the summertime intense thunderstorms occasionally occur that blast the mountains with lightning and cause flash floods....

Black clouds hovered over the lofty cliffs of Red Rock Canyon, and a fierce storm punctuated by lightning and thunder echoed through the canyons. Lightning flashed and struck the rocky cliffs causing pieces of rock to go crashing down into the wash below.

On one ledge, after millions of years of erosion removed the overlying rock, several roundish objects - very different than the surrounding sandstone - were exposed. These objects were eggs laid by a dinosaur that lived 190 million years ago when Southern Nevada was a vast desert with towering sand dunes. Only the toughest dinosaurs could survive in the hostile hot and dry terrain.

Lightning struck one of the dinosaur eggs with 100 million volts of electricity...

...and when the dust cleared, something was moving - a little boy dinosaur was hatched!

When the storm ended, the young dinosaur began searching for his family. On a ledge higher up on the mountain a bighorn sheep was watching....

The young dinosaur began roaming the rugged terrain that had steep slopes, rocky outcrops, cacti, and other thorny plants and trees. He met an orange lizard covered with bumps.

"What are you, and how do you survive in this desert?" asked the young dinosaur.

The lizard replied, "I am a Gila monster, and I live here in these rocks. Most animals are afraid of me because my bite is poisonous. I survive by burrowing in the ground and staying there most of the time, coming out only to find food and water."

"Am I a Gila monster?" asked the dinosaur.

"No, you are not a Gila monster. I don't know what you are," answered the Gila monster.

The young dinosaur moved on. He went into a rocky area with many cracks and crevices in the rocks. He met another lizard, less fearsome-looking than the Gila monster, and said,

"Hello, what are you?"

"I am a chuckwalla, and I like to hide in the cracks in the rocks and boulders."

"You are not as scary looking as the Gila monster. What do you do if an enemy wants to eat you?" asked the dinosaur.

"I go into an opening in the rock and inflate my body so it is wedged in the crack - nothing can pull me out. And I stay there until they leave," said the chuckwalla.

"Am I a chuckwalla?" asked the dinosaur.

"No, you are not a chuckwalla. I don't know what you are," said the chuckwalla.

Becoming sad and lonely, the young dinosaur continued to roam the rugged, rocky country looking for his family. He saw a slow-moving creature. It was a reptile, but not a lizard.

"Hello, what are you?" asked the dinosaur, "And how can you survive here if you move so slow?"

"I am a desert tortoise, and if anything attacks me I pull my head and feet into this hard and tough shell and wait until they move on," answered the tortoise.

"How do you cope with the summer heat and winter cold?" asked the dinosaur.

"I go into my burrow during the heat of the day in the summer, and go to sleep in my burrow during the winter months," answered the tortoise.

"Am I a desert tortoise?" asked the dinosaur.

"No, you are not a desert tortoise. I don't know what you are," answered the tortoise.

The dinosaur and desert tortoise watched as a bighorn sheep came down the ledges and approached the dinosaur. He nodded hello to the tortoise and said to the dinosaur,

"I have been watching you and listening to you. I have something to show you, but you have to be very brave. Follow me."

The tortoise told the dinosaur that the bighorn watches everything that goes on from his high perch and knows all that happens in Red Rock Canyon.

"You should go with him," said the tortoise.

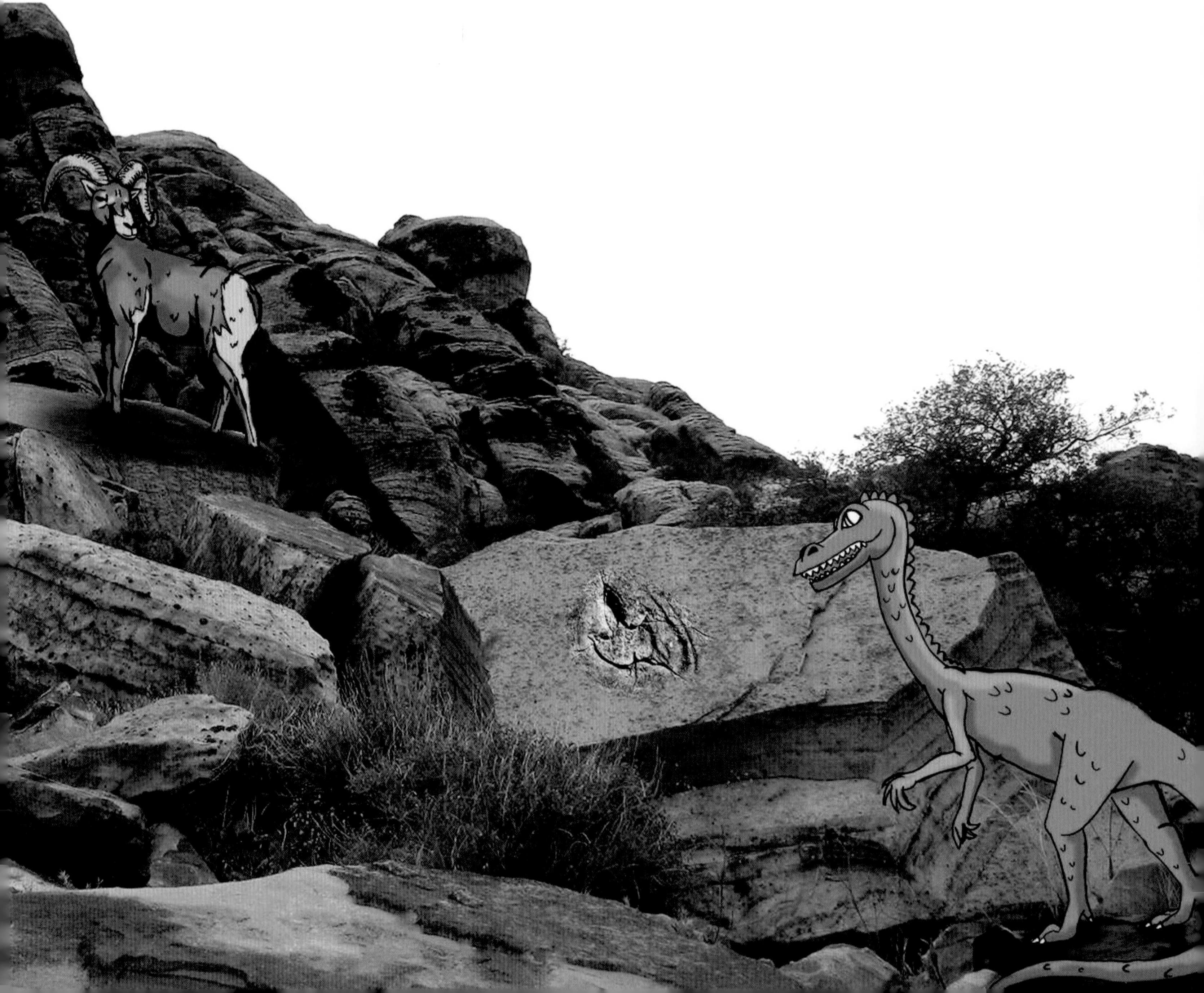

The young dinosaur said goodbye to the tortoise and began following the bighorn up the ledges. Following the bighorn, the dinosaur discovered tracks - a dinosaur footprint- in the sandstone, just like his own.

"My family must be close - I can see their tracks!" he shouted happily to the bighorn.

"No," the bighorn said, "those tracks in the rock are very, very old. Keep following me."

The bighorn moved on, higher and higher up the rocky ledges, the young dinosaur following sadly behind. He could tell that he could never reach the heights that the bighorn could reach and was relieved when the bighorn stopped at a smooth, steeply-sloping ledge.

And now the young dinosaur understood why the bighorn told him to be brave. It was not because of the steep climb up the rocks. There, on the ledge, embedded in the rock, were the remains of an animal - a fossil - that looked like him.

"There is all that remains of your family. You are a dinosaur, and your kind has not been seen in Red Rock Canyon for millions of years. Dinosaurs used to rule the Earth, now humans rule," said the bighorn.

"How do you know this?" asked the young dinosaur, unable to take his teary eyes off the fossil dinosaur remains embedded in the rock.

"A few months ago I overheard two geologists talking right here," answered the bighorn.

"What are geologists?" asked the dinosaur.

"Geologists are humans who study rocks and who are always snooping around on the rocky ledges," said the bighorn.

The young dinosaur was sadder and lonelier than ever. He thanked the bighorn and began moving down the slope through the rugged rock formations, back to the area where he was born. He was as alone as a creature could be, with no family, and most of his new friends being desert dwellers of a different species. Most of them burrowed in the ground or hid in the rocks for long periods of time.

Dark clouds began to gather again in Red Rock Canyon, and another fierce summer thunderstorm began. Lightning flashed, and claps of thunder echoed through the canyons.

They say that lightning never strikes twice in the same place. But this time it almost did. It struck a ledge just above the sandstone layer where the dinosaur eggs were exposed. More dinosaur eggs were embedded in the sandstone on this ledge. The young boy dinosaur watched in awe as lightning hit an exposed egg…

...and a female dinosaur was hatched!

But the rain accompanying the lightning was intense and flash flooding began to occur. The little girl dinosaur was swept off her feet by the running water and was carried to a "dry waterfall" - a rocky cliff in the usually dry wash channel. Only now it was a real waterfall, with water gushing over it. The boy dinosaur moved quickly and plucked her from the torrent - he saved her life.

As they looked at each other affectionately, the storm cleared and a beautiful rainbow appeared over Red Rock Canyon. They walked off together leaving footprints in the wet sandy mud....

A couple of days later two hikers came upon the footprints in the sun-dried mud.

"Hey, look at these tracks - they almost look like dinosaur tracks," said one hiker.

The other hiker replied, "Probably some birds like a Golden Eagle or Turkey Vulture or something. But wouldn't that be cool if dinosaurs were living today in Red Rock Canyon?!"

The End

Turtlehead Books

1587 Figueroa Drive

Las Vegas, NV 89123

(702) 896-4049

Greatunc@aol.com